The bears were longing to get b in business. Once they had been the "Shoe Shop Bears"; they had even taken their names from the boxes in the shop —Boots, Slippers, and Socks. It had been very satisfying to be placed in the arms of children to pacify them while their new shoes were being tried on. Later, when Polly the shoe clerk took the bears home to live, they were delighted to be part of her family.

But now they were beginning to grow restless. "You need fresh interests," Hannibal the elephant told them. "For bears with your business experience, something's bound to turn up."

Something did turn up while Socks, the youngest bear, was sitting one day in a toy car on the sidewalk. A coal truck stopped in front of the house, and a toy monkey, who was fastened to the front of the truck as mascot, leaned over to speak to Socks. "If it's a ride you're after," he confided, "why don't you come down to the station for their beloved Polly.

MARGARET J. BAKER lives in Somerset, England, in a house called "The Hare and Hounds," which was once an inn. She has written two earlier books about the bears: *The Shoe Shop Bears* and *Hannibal and the Bears*. Miss Baker's other books for young readers include *Castaway Christmas*, *Homer the Tortoise*, and *Away Went Galloper*.

Bears Back in Business

Margaret J. Baker has also written

Bears Back in Business

by MARGARET J. BAKER

Illustrated by
DAPHNE ROWLES

FARRAR, STRAUS & GIROUX
AN ARIEL BOOK | NEW YORK

Contents

Bears Back in Business

The Sales Drive

"You would have thought someone might have come," Slippers said as she and the other two teddy bears sat in the kitchen of No. 1, Station Road before the circle of doll's teacups set out on the hearthrug before the fire. "With orangeade for the younger ones in the fish-paste jars, we could have managed two dozen at least."

"And it's not as if we hadn't asked everybody," said Socks, the smallest bear. "All the corn merchant's

3

tabbies and that new cat called Bret at the garage, besides Big Tom and Little Tom from the cathedral and Hobson at the grocer's."

Boots frowned at the youngest bear before he reminded Slippers of their other friends among the cats in Slumber Lightly who had failed to accept her invitation. Like the other bears, Boots was no longer new. The big bear's fur had grown thin around his muzzle and the pads on his paws had been carefully repaired with chamois leather stitched on with cobbler's thread. Once Boots and Slippers and Socks had worked in the shoe shop in Cordwainer's Row, where they had helped amuse the children during the fitting of their shoes. After their retirement several years ago, Polly Trinket, the young assistant in the shoe shop, had taken them home to amuse her own younger brothers and sister in the terrace house in Station Road.

No one could have looked after the bears better than Simon and Bill and Audrey Trinket, but now the two boys were both at the cathedral choir school, and their sister was at a comprehensive school on the far side of the cathedral town. Polly, their elder sister, was always busy at the shoe shop, and their mother worked for most of the day in a café in the town. Left alone in the house, there was little for the bears to do. Even Boots had to admit they were often bored.

"It is the third tea party we've given this week,"

4

he pointed out, "not counting that night Hobson dropped in with Big Tom and Little Tom and we asked them to stay. No one likes a chat and a sit down more than Hobson, but as the only cat at the grocer's he can't be away while they're stock-taking. When the tea chests and cartons are shifted, anything may turn up, and the younger assistants are jumpy if he's not at hand."

"Last year Hobson says there was a whole nest of mice, cheeky as you like, behind the cartons of Wonder White detergent," added Socks. "They'd used a crate of giveaway plastic flowers for cover and raised two families before Hobson was on to them. There was a chase right down Cordwainer's Row. Several of the smallest went to ground in the television shop and they've caused no end of trouble in the sets which are sent out to rent. Two others bolted into the church fittings shop. Big Tom says sooner or later they're bound to turn up with supplies for the cathedral. He and Little Tom are on the lookout every time there's a delivery of new hassocks."

Hobson, the large black and white cat from the grocer's shop next to the shoe shop where the bears had once been employed, and Big Tom and Little Tom, the two lean mousers from the cathedral, were among the bears' oldest friends in Slumber Lightly. Slippers knew Boots and Socks were right. Their friends had stayed away from her tea party not from choice but because they were working cats and busy with their daily duties. Yet, looking at the empty places, she sighed. The cups were set on a lace table-cloth made from the biggest mat of the duchesse set used on the spare-room dressing table. Silver paper covered the cake plates, and toffee wrapping papers were folded beside each place instead of napkins. If the tea party had been a success, Slippers had decided to go one better the following week with a running buffet which she had seen described in one of Polly Trinket's favorite magazines.

"Apart from Boots, none of us can walk much," Socks had objected when she told him of her plan, "so I don't see how we would really enjoy a party where we had to run."

And Boots had enjoyed explaining to the younger bear that a running buffet was a special meal at which guests helped themselves from dishes set on a side-board.

"Boots and I have come anyway," said Socks cheer-fully, interrupting her thoughts, "and Hannibal will be in as soon as he wakes up. Even if he never says much, he likes to be with us, and with his wheeled platform he really needs an extra place."

Hannibal was a large stuffed elephant who was older than them all. On his wheeled platform, he usu-

ally spent the afternoon standing in the hall. The
sunlight shone through the ruby and gold glass in
the front door on his patched gray coat and crimson
saddlecloth, which was edged with gold lampshade
fringe and brass cat bells. Dozing there, Hannibal was
content. He was an honored member of the house-
hold. However busy the children were, Bill and
Simon never failed to oil Hannibal's wheels, or
Audrey to stitch one of the cat bells back on if it

7

was hanging loose. Apart from an old doll's carriage, which Boots could push in an emergency, Hannibal was the bears' only means of transport. On misty autumn mornings he would take them for an outing around the town. Slippers and Socks sat on his back while Boots held the handle of Hannibal's platform and pushed. Sometimes they went as far as Cordwainer's Row and waved to Hobson as he sat beside a bag of coffee beans in the grocer's shop window, or they would greet Big Tom and Little Tom as they left the cathedral and padded across the cobweb-spun green to the Sexton's lodge for breakfast.

With the bears and Hannibal gathered around her, Slippers soon forgot her disappointment. Some days before, she had noticed a moth asleep on Boots's shoulder and she had insisted on Boots's visiting the dry cleaner's, hidden in a bundle of the boys' winter overcoats. Boots told the others about it while they had tea.

"Quite like old times it was," he said. "After the cleaning was done, I was put in the shop window with two eiderdowns that had been re-covered and several felt hats. Miss Frazer, who looks after the shop, was good enough to say I brought in a fair amount of extra trade. They had done a most thorough job and my fur came up like gold."

Slippers stared proudly at the big bear. Her own

honey-colored fur was worn as smooth as the downy lining of a broad bean pod, her nose and mouth were marked in with brown darning wool, and one of her ears was missing altogether, but Boots was still a most handsome and upstanding bear. Boots had enjoyed his work in the shoe shop more than any of them, and although their retirement had been so happy, Slippers knew how much Boots sometimes missed the interest of his old life.

"The dry-cleaning shop wouldn't need anyone permanent I suppose?" she asked. "Their moth-proofing methods couldn't be bettered and it's no more than a step, so you would be home every night."

Boots looked down into his teacup.

"I did ask the young tabby who lives over the shop and looks in about eleven when the assistant makes the tea," he said. "Unfortunately, their head office likes them to change the window display frequently. One week it's lampshades and soft furnishings, and the next, suède coats and lamb's-wool jackets."

"Then I should try somewhere else," said Hannibal, looking up. "It's high time you all had a change. You need fresh interests. For bears with your business experience, something's bound to turn up."

"You mean we all ought to go back to work?" asked Slippers. Socks stared.

"Part-time at least," said Hannibal. "Now that the

children are older, there's nothing to stop you, and Socks would find it a good deal more fun."

Once the bears had decided to follow Hannibal's advice and find fresh employment, all their friends among the cats in Slumber Lightly did what they could to help.

Hobson from the grocer's was most encouraging about their chances.

"There are fresh openings in the town every day now," he told them. "The dry-goods store has a new white bear for their baby-clothes display, and there are several more on the hosiery counter."

The cats from the cathedral were full of enthusiasm also.

"We heard yesterday of a vacancy at the airport," Big Tom reported. "The airline hostesses like to keep a bear handy for the younger travelers on all their flights, and they need a replacement for their Far Eastern route."

"As soon as we heard about it, we thought of Boots," added Little Tom. "And things are always happening to the airline bears, so they'll be bound to fit you all in quite soon."

At the sight of Slippers's face, and of Socks already jumping up and down with excitement, Hobson frowned at the two cats.

"It would be most unsuitable and quite out of the

question," he said shortly. "Boots and the others still have some responsibilities at home, and during the school holidays there's no telling where they might be—over the Persian Gulf or the North Pole."

The bears heard of a more suitable opening through another of their friends, a half-Persian cat called Fluffy, who worked at the local movie house. One of her many relations was a young ginger cat owned by the head buyer at the biggest store in the town.

"It's only seasonal work for their toy bazaar at Christmas," she explained, "but there might be possibilities."

Boots set off for the store with a label from a mail-order catalogue pinned to his chest, saying that the same model was also available in medium or small sizes.

When Boots returned, they knew at once that he had met with no success.

"Fluffy's young relation was very civil," Boots told the other bears in answer to their questions. "She took me in by the back way straight to the toy department, and the manager looked me over with the other yuletide novelties at the coffee break."

"And what did he say?" asked Socks.

Boots stared at his back paws.

"Just that they weren't so pushed for toys for their window display that they needed to use toys from the year one," said Boots. "Though probably we're well out of it. We should have had to sit in the window all day having tea with two dolls and a rather forward young bear with ginger plastic pads on his paws, dark glasses, and a paper cap."

For some time afterward, the bears went on with their old way of life. Boots read old copies of the *Boot and Shoe Gazette* and compared the advantages of cleaning shoes with a wax pad applicator over putting on polish from a can, using an old sock. Slippers worried about Socks, who was restless and naughty.

In the evening, the children were busy with homework, and Polly Trinket was seldom at home after the shoe shop was shut.

On her dressing table stood the photograph of a young man with a bush of red hair and a pale freckled face. *"Yours ever, Franklin Fielding"* was written very straight across the corner.

"He's a salesman for youths' and gentlemen's footwear," Boots explained. "Hobson says he's in and out of Polly's shoe shop once or twice a month. Most of the choristers at the cathedral wear his firm's Oxford shoes now, which are guaranteed waterproof, and have microcellular soles."

"Mrs. Trinket's new winter snow boots must have been made by his company too," said Socks. "I heard him tell Polly that with the tough rubber soles they were an extra good line and wonderful value."

"Very likely," said Boots shortly. "All their foot-wear's sound enough, though not to be compared with the quality stuff the old manager had in the shop when we first went there."

On Sundays, Frank Fielding always came to tea. He wore his best dark blue suit and talked to Polly about the latest fashions in men's footwear, with names like Chukka and Chelsea boots and Cavalry casuals, which even Boots had never heard of.

"Probably the Trinkets asked him around because he lives in lodgings and it's too far for him to go home for the weekend," Slippers suggested.

"It's more than that," insisted Boots. "They're courting! When they've saved up enough money, they'll get married."

Slippers stared.

"But Polly's pretty enough to marry anyone. It ought to be a prince at least. Even if there aren't enough English ones to go around, one from abroad would do."

"Or a really handsome cowboy who would let her ride his horse," said Socks. "Not someone like Frank who has colds that need Friar's Balsam, and that boil on the back of his neck Mrs. Trinket had to look after, and hair that won't stay flat."

"Polly likes looking after people," said Boots gloomily. "Look how she took to us."

On Sunday afternoons, Frank often took all the family out in the small delivery truck he used for business.

"Even with all the shoe boxes cleared out of the back, they're pressed for room," Slippers remarked as they watched the delivery truck drive away. "We couldn't expect Frank to take us as well."

In spite of her words, the bears often felt low when left alone in the empty house during the long November afternoons. Slippers knew Socks longed for a ride more than any of them. In summer, Hannibal would have taken them out, but now the weather was too uncertain.

"Once Hannibal's wet through, it takes ages for him to dry out," Slippers told the small bear. "With straw stuffing like his, there's always the danger of mold setting in."

The bears were alone on just such a Sunday afternoon when the two cathedral mousers arrived with news of work for them all.

"We knew you'd almost given up hope of finding anything suitable," said Big Tom, "but we thought this was a chance you wouldn't want to let slip."

"Once the news is out, there will be dozens after the jobs, so I'd go around tomorrow at eight sharp," advised Little Tom.

"You'd be needed to take part in an autumn sales drive to sell solid fuel," explained his companion. "The coalman mentioned it to the sexton when he delivered the last of the cut-price coke for the cathedral boilers."

"The coal merchants need three teddy bears to ride on one of their railroad coal cars," explained Big Tom. "It's to remind people of the comfort of an open coal fire."

"And make them order an extra ton of Derby Brights or Best Kitchen Nuts," said Little Tom.

"The fact that none of you are new shouldn't go against you," said Big Tom. "What they have in mind is three bears who look comfortable and homey. The manager doesn't want to splash out and make a great outlay. 'Something reasonably presentable' is what the coalman said he's after."

"So we thought of you at once," said Little Tom. "Slackworthy and Poke-it is the name of the firm, and their office is on the far side of the railroad station."

The bears had never felt so excited. Slippers brushed them so hard their fur flew out, and Socks never stopped talking about the sales drive till they went to bed. He started again the second they woke on Monday morning.

"Where do you think we'll go in the coal car?" he asked.

"A sales drive might be to anywhere," Boots explained as he struggled into his best red jumper, which had shrunk in the wash. "Probably it will be rather like one of those whistle-stop tours they have before choosing their new president in America."

"But none of us can make speeches," said Socks as Slippers rubbed a stain of dark tan shoe polish from his paw with an old toothbrush, "so what will we do instead?"

"Wave, most likely, as the car goes by," said Slippers. "No one would expect any more, and we'll take the sand-castle flags so that everyone can see."

Hannibal saw them off from the washhouse door. They had decided to travel in the old doll's carriage to save Hannibal waiting about. Out of doors it was still almost dark and very cold.

"You shouldn't have got up so early," Slippers told the old elephant. "Even Mrs. Trinket isn't down yet."

"I'll have another nap when you've gone," said Hannibal. "There will be plenty of time."

"Wherever we're off to, we're sure to be back in a day or so," said Boots.

"Unless we don't suit," said Slippers. "Then it will be almost at once."

"Of course you'll suit," said Hannibal. "With your experience in trade, they're lucky to have you."

With Hannibal's words ringing in their ears, Boots

pushed the carriage down the misty road. Even Socks didn't grumble about the wobbly wheels and slow trundle of the old carriage because he knew that soon they would be speeding along in a railway car of their own.

The streets near the station were crowded with trucks of all kinds. Twice Boots had to pause outside a candy shop so that passers-by would imagine he and the others had been left outside by a young customer.

They found the coal merchant's office with no difficulty and Boots trundled the carriage down a passage that smelled of the same kitchen nuts that were burned on the stove at home. Several milk bottles stood beside a window marked *Inquiries*. The bears waited beside them while Boots rang the bell.

A moment later, a boy poked his head through the window and stared at the bears. He was so close they could smell hair oil mixed with extra-strong peppermint chewing gum.

"There's three bears out here with the milk for the tea," he called. "What shall I do with them? Whoever left them has run off."

Inside the office, the sound of a typewriter never faltered.

"Those will be the teddy bears for Mr. Slackworthy's display," said the typist. "Bring them

18

straight in, Sidney, and leave them on my desk for him to see."

From the top of the typist's desk the bears inspected the office. It was tidy and bare. Only three piles of coke, coal, and anthracite decorated the mantle, but the bears' eyes were fixed on the window, through which they could see the railway siding where several coal cars stood, with *Slackworthy and Poke-it* painted on their sides.

"They're loaded up already and coupled to the engine," whispered Socks. "I expect the train's only waiting for us to go on board."

Beside him, Slippers shivered. The coal cars looked far larger than she had imagined. She wondered how they would hold on when they were perched on the large lumps of coal, and what would happen about soot when they thundered through a tunnel. Boots edged closer to her side and rested his paw on her own.

No one paid any more attention to the bears. The typist worked so fast that once the carriage of her typewriter toppled Boots over as he peered at an invoice she was typing for boiler fuel. Socks, who was leaning against him, also lost his balance and sat down on the rather wet saucer of the typist's teacup. She set him to dry on a piece of blotting paper and went on with her work.

"If you're the least bit damp, change places with me and sit by the radiator," Slippers whispered, but a short dark man, who they guessed must be Mr. Slackworthy, bustled into the room before she could fuss any more. He frowned when he noticed the bears, and they held their breath.

"Run along with these to the display car at once," he told the office boy. "By rights we should have had them on it hours ago. With a sales drive to catch the public's eye, it's detail and speed that we have to watch."

The boy tucked the bears under his arm and hurried down the corridor. For a moment the bears heard the roar of the traffic, then swinging doors closed behind them and they saw that they were in a brightly lit showroom.

As the boy carried them across the showroom, Socks stiffened in his arms and the other bears stared.

Ahead of them in the shop window, a small-scale railroad track was laid, and on it stood a model coal car loaded with lumps of coal. Behind the car was a banner on which was painted the slogan:

BE COZY AS OUR BEARS!
BUY MORE COAL AT CUT PRICES
DURING OUR AUTUMN SALES DRIVE!

The bears did not speak or even look at one another

as the office boy set them on top of the piled coal in the car, with the sand-castle flags tucked under their arms. They knew that any journey they made in the coal car could never be farther than the length of the shop window, bordered by a knitting-wool and embroidery shop on one side and the office of Slackworthy and Poke-it on the other.

Socks waved his flag and blinked back the tears he was too proud to shed. He stared through the plate-glass window at the busy traffic. It was then that he saw the toy rabbit perched on the radiator of a large blue and gold delivery truck. While the van was stopped opposite the shop window, Socks just had time to notice the small rabbit's stiff body covered with mud-spattered fur, his bright button eyes set in a small pointed mask, and his stand-up ears lined with oil-stained material that might once have been pink. As Socks stared, the rabbit spotted him. He raised his arm in a cheerful greeting before the traffic rumbled forward and he was gone.

Winks on the Dodge

"Naturally we worked out the week," Boots explained to Hobson, "but it was a dead-end job and it would never have done to stay. Mr. Slackworthy saw it wasn't practical himself. Even though we sat on Coal Board leaflets, our fur was pot black by the end of the day. He's put in an order now for plastic daffodils for the spring, and until they put a sprinkling of artificial snow and holly on the car for the festive season, he'll make do with a picture of some koala bears and two prickly-pear cactuses from his own greenhouse."

"I've not got the worst of the coal dust off Socks yet," said Slippers. "Hannibal said the little fellow put him in mind of a golliwog they'd had in his first nursery."

"Big Tom and Little Tom should have known better than to have sent you there in the first place," said Hobson. "They have no real knowledge of business or trade and it would have been far better if they hadn't interfered. Something really suitable is bound to turn up in time. For the moment I should just take things easy."

Boots and Slippers were content to follow Hobson's advice. Frank Fielding took Polly's young brothers to several football games, and Boots went too, wearing a large rosette and a scarf knitted in the home team's colors. Sometimes he tried to play football with Socks while Hannibal guarded the goal, but the smaller bear was restless and soon lost interest.

Socks spent hours with his nose pressed to the window, watching the traffic. Once the big black and white cat from the grocer's came upon Socks upside down in the gutter almost on the main street.

"He'd taken one of the boys' roller skates," Slippers told Hannibal after she and Boots had dusted the small bear down and put him to bed. "Hobson said he'd been riding on it head first and holding on by the strap. If Hobson hadn't come by, anything might have happened."

"Give him time and I'm sure he'll settle down," said Hannibal. "He never said much, but that job at the coal merchant's must have been a great disappoint-

ment to him. You and Boots will have to make allow-
ances."

One foggy afternoon late in November, Socks was
playing with a toy truck on the front steps when a
coal truck stopped outside the house.

"You won't go far in that," said a voice, and looking up, Socks saw a toy monkey grinning at him from
the head of the coal truck. "If it's a ride you're after,
why don't you come down to the station yard and let
Winks on the Dodge fix you up? He's always there
with the rest of us about now. I'm Joshua on the Tipper. My truck's fitted with a hydraulic tipper especially for coal. As soon as this lot's delivered, we'll be
off back to the yard and you could come along with
us."

Socks hesitated. Joshua's hat was set at an angle and
trimmed with a red feather snapped off at the tip. His
yellow jacket was blackened with coal dust and oil.
He held on to the bars of the grille with one long
arm. The other he extended for Socks to catch hold
of.

"How would I come back?" Socks asked. "I'm not
much good at walking."

Joshua laughed so that all his teeth showed.

"Walking—why, none of us even try! What's the
point, when there are wheels? Riding's the thing! So
long as there are vans and trucks on the road, who'd
choose to walk? Winks and the rest of us haven't

bothered for years. In the town, someone's always going your way. Feathers on the mail truck, Watchit on the newspaper truck, and Upsidaisy on the British Road Services parcels truck cover most of the streets. Not to speak of Bits on the municipal road sweeper, Tallyho on the telephones, Plush on the Leyland

eight-wheeler, and Winks here, there, and everywhere on the Dodge."

Socks blinked and edged nearer to the coal truck. Behind him, Slippers dozed on the windowsill of the front room. In the kitchen, Boots was studying a textbook on footwear manufacture which Frank Fielding had lent to Polly. Now and then, Boots read a bit about galloon trimmings or Albert Tab slippers aloud to Hannibal, who said, "Just fancy!" or "Would you believe it!" without opening his eyes. Socks knew the book contained over six hundred pages and should keep Boots occupied for some time.

"Come on, if you're going to!" urged Joshua. "That's the last bag of kitchen nuts going in now."

Joshua grabbed Socks's paw as he jumped from the high curb. A moment later, Socks was on the bumper of the truck, wedged behind a fog light.

"Don't any of you ever fall off?" Socks asked as the truck moved forward and the wind whistled in his ears.

"Not if Winks can help it," said Joshua, steadying the bear with his free arm. "He doesn't hold with risks just for the thrill of them. All the mascots are divided into three sorts—'bumpers,' 'hoods,' and 'cabbies'—according to where we ride. Winks can always judge who's up to riding outside or who's liable to turn dizzy and ought to go in the cab. On the whole, he's usually right and it's best to do as he says."

"He sounds a bit bossy," objected Socks. "Why do you let him tell you what to do so much?"

"Because he's been on the road longer than any of us," said Joshua shortly. "What Winks doesn't know about road haulage wouldn't cover a sixpence. Cracker, that's his driver, had him right through the war. They've stuck together ever since."

It was dusk when they turned in to the station yard. Lights glowed from the ticket-office window. Down the line, the traffic lights shone through the mist.

"There are always a good many trucks and vans in about now," Joshua told Socks as the coal truck drew up alongside a battered newspaper truck and an eight-wheeler. "The London train's due and most of the drivers have a cup of tea with the porters while they're waiting."

Socks wasn't listening. His eyes were set on a large blue and gold van waiting by the freight depot. He was sure it was the same as the van he had seen from the coal merchant's shop window. Even as he stared, the small rabbit fixed to the grille lifted his paw in greeting.

"I'll take you over to Winks at once," Joshua told Socks as he helped him scramble to the ground. "You can meet the others later on."

Beside him, Socks hesitated. After his first ride, he

felt wobbly on his feet. All around the yard the eyes of the other mascots were turned upon him.

"Couldn't I have a word with that rabbit on the big blue van first?" he asked. "He waved to me once before, when his van was held up in a traffic jam."

Joshua turned to him with a grin.

WINKS

"But that *is* Winks, he said, "up on the Dodge."

Winks was smaller than Socks. On the hood of the big delivery van, the rabbit looked even smaller. From the tips of his up-raised ears to his back paws he measured exactly six inches, but he stood up very straight and his body was stoutly made. Slung on a length of string across his chest was a metal watering can which had come from a Christmas party snapper. Winks's fur was worn down nearly to the fine-meshed gold canvas, and one of his legs was sewn on with black thread. The stitches were large and his leg wobbled loosely, as if he was always dancing a highland fling. The small rabbit's black button eyes were friendly as he looked down at Socks.

"Glad you've found your way," he said. "When I saw you in the coal merchant's window, I guessed that the job didn't suit and that you might be along."

Even with Winks to prompt him, Socks was confused by the names of all the different mascots on the vans and trucks gathered in the station yard.

"You'll get the hang of us soon enough," Winks told him as he showed Socks around. "Just catch on to a name here and there. Ours are mostly nicknames we've picked up on the road. No one will fuss if you make mistakes at first."

Once they had stopped being curious, all the animals were friendly and proud to show Socks their vehicles.

A pink rabbit with bright blue eyes and curled whiskers greeted them from the cab of the large eight-wheeler Leyland truck.

"Pleased to meet you, I'm sure," she said, looking down at her front paws as she sat in a corner behind the curved windshield.

"That's Plush," explained Winks. "She's as pleasant a young rabbit as you could wish to meet. She was made as a hygienic toy to travel in a baby's carriage. Long-distance road haulage is a very different cup of tea, but Plush has taken to it like a duck to water. There's hardly a highway in the country she hasn't traveled on, and she's made the cab of that Leyland like a home away from home, with everything spotless, and artificial flowers in one of those plastic cone vases stuck to the dashboard."

Helped by Joshua and Winks, Socks scrambled from one vehicle to the next. He met Watchit on the

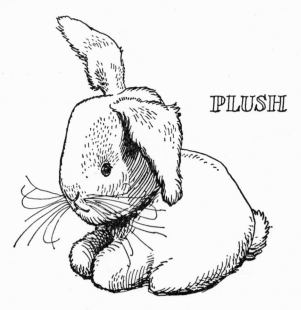

PLUSH

newspaper truck, Tallyho on the telephone repair truck, Upsidaisy on the British Road Services parcels truck, and Feathers on the post-office mail truck.

The mascots were all busy and cheerful. Bright feathers and bits of ribbon or colored tape decorated their mud-stained fur. Often fastened beside them on

UPSIDAISY

the radiators or bumpers of the vans and trucks was a silver cardboard horseshoe, or a bunch of dried heather. One or two of the mascots were dolls with battered wind-blown wigs and eyes that swung open and shut. Upsidaisy, who rode on the hood of the parcels truck, had once been an ornamental doll pincushion on a lady's dressing table. Now her taffeta crinoline and the stand it had covered were missing. Only Upsidaisy's ringleted head and sloping china shoulders and arms remained. From the waist downward, she was wrapped around in a spotted red handkerchief which clashed rather badly with her faded lilac silk bodice.

"Not having her crinoline and the stand doesn't bother Upsidaisy a bit," Winks explained when Socks asked. "The stand was only stuffed with sawdust, and though it didn't show under her crinoline, she never had any feet in the first place. Stuck on a dressing table all day, she had a pretty dull time, and nowadays she travels all over the town."

The only mascot who seemed gloomy was Watchit, a pug dog made of grubby light blue velvet, who rode on the bumper of the newspaper truck. "There must be more uncomfortable ways of earning a living," he told Socks. "Only, just for the moment I can't bring one to mind."

"Watchit's always like that," Winks explained. "Once he's racing around the town with an extra edition of a newspaper to deliver in double-quick time, no one could enjoy the work more. That van of his has a fine turn of speed and is as nippy as you could wish in the rush-hour traffic. Once, a news agent's little girl took a fancy to Watchit and had him off the van to push him in her doll's carriage and lay him to sleep with her other toys in a cot, but Watchit couldn't stand it. He was back on the van within the week."

"You see, when he was new, Watchit was sold as a mascot for Cambridge at the boat race," explained Joshua. "That year Oxford won, and Watchit's never really got over it."

"He took it very hard," said Winks, "and it doesn't help when the others tease him and say, 'Which boat race?' as if they've never heard of the one that's rowed each year on the Thames by crews from the universities of Oxford and Cambridge."

After their tour, Socks sat with the others in a corner of the yard. The vans and trucks towered above them. Over the railroad station the sky was pricked with stars. The light from a truck's taillights glowed on the faces of his new friends.

"Traveling on the trucks is rough in a bad winter, I grant you," said Winks. "I've been coated with ice many a time, and the wind cuts right through you when you're up on the hood going full pelt down a highway, but it's a good open-air life. You'll have to judge for yourself. If you still have a fancy for it after a few runs around the town, you could come

33

out with me on the Dodge and I'll see how you shape up."

Slippers missed Socks at tea.

"I've searched everywhere," she told Boots when she found him asleep with his head on the textbook. "Hannibal says the last time he saw Socks he was playing with that old toy truck on the front step. I found the truck upside down by the shoe scraper, but there's not a sign of Socks."

"Then we'd better take Hannibal and search down the street," said Boots.

As they paused outside the house looking up and down the lamp-lit street, a mail truck rounded the corner and sped toward them. Slippers clutched Boots's arm and Hannibal blinked. Socks was riding on the bumper of the truck with his back paws dangling over the license plate. At his side, waving gaily to them all, was another small bear. Two silver bells hung around her neck on a piece of tattered satin ribbon, and by the light of the headlights they saw that her fur had once been white.

"It's me!" Socks shouted as the truck drew up and the postman alighted to clear the letter box. "Feathers has brought me up from the yard. We'd have been here sooner, only there were a good many other boxes to clear first."

The white bear giggled as Socks scrambled down,

and Boots only just saved him from slipping through the bars of a drain grating in the gutter.

"Socks might have been riding on the trucks all his life instead of one afternoon," she said. "Coming down the High Street, he was all for trying with no hands."

"Feathers was once on an engagement-ring stand in a jeweler's shop window," said Socks. "Those bells she wears came from the orange-blossom arch where she stood. The stand turned around and around, but she likes being on the truck much better."

"Shop work would fair fidget me now!" said Feathers, tinkling her bells as she balanced on the bumper with the engine vibrating behind her.

"What suits one doesn't suit another," said Slippers shortly. "But it was good of you to bring Socks back."

"Any time," said Feathers lightly as the postman banged the door of the truck, which then went on its way with a flash of red paint.

"Now you'd better tell us exactly where you've been and what you were doing," Boots told Socks as he led him indoors.

"Slippers has been worried out of her wits," added Hannibal severely. "None of the Trinkets would have been allowed to go off like that or accept lifts from perfect strangers."

"I'm sorry you've been worried," said Socks when

they stood in the kitchen, "but I've only been as far as the station yard to meet Winks and the other mascots who ride on the trucks. Joshua on the coal truck took me, and it was one of Slackworthy and Poke-it's, so I knew it was all right. Winks says so long as you're sensible and don't lark about, riding on the trucks is as safe as houses. He laughed like anything when I told him the bother we'd always had traveling about."

Slippers tugged an old antifreeze *Do-not-drain-this-tank* sticker from Socks's back paw and brushed the worst of the mud off his fur with the hearth brush.

"I'm sure with Hannibal and the doll's carriage we've managed very well up to now," she said. "Hannibal and Boots have always been most obliging."

"Of course they have," said Socks somewhat jerkily as Slippers scrubbed at an oil smudge on his face with a piece of flannel. "Only this way, Winks says distance is no object. You're free to travel anywhere— around the town on a milk truck or the municipal sweeper or all the way to Scotland on a furniture van."

Socks didn't stop talking about the trucks and his new friends all that evening. Even when Boots was watching his favorite detective serial on television, Socks continually interrupted to whisper: "That van the police are using while they wait for the burglars is a Commer . . . That's an articulated tractor, with a trailer blocking their view . . . Those trucks the burglars have ready for their getaway carry ten tons. Winks says they're exported to all parts of the world."

Even in bed, Socks repeated in a sleepy singsong the names of all his new friends and the vehicles they rode on.

"Joshua on the Tipper, Upsidaisy on the British Road Services parcels truck, Watchit on the newspaper truck, Plush on the Leyland, Feathers on the mail truck, and Winks on the Dodge."

"He's asleep now," Slippers reported to Boots after she had gone to tuck him in. "I've never seen Socks so taken with anything before. The last thing he asked me was if he might go down to the station yard again. The coal truck will be around with a load of coke tomorrow, so this Joshua would give him a lift and apparently Socks has been told that he's welcome to drop in any time he likes."

"And what did you say?" asked Boots.

"That we'd see," said Slippers, staring into the fire with an anxious face. "Naturally we'll have to make inquiries, but if this is what he wants, I don't think we should stand in his way."

Not Really a Party

"You couldn't find a better bunch of animals than those who travel on the road," Hobson assured Boots and Slippers when they asked the grocer's cat about Socks's new friends. "Scruffy and muddy they may be, with a fancy for gaudy ribbons and clothes, but they stick together and Socks will come to no harm with them. Winks I've known for years. Rain or shine, he's always been ready with a cheerful word when his van has been in the Row. He'll keep an eye on Socks, and you should feel proud they've taken a fancy to him, for they're a clannish, choosy lot and it's not often an outsider is made so welcome."

Even the two mousers from the cathedral approved.

"To be out and about with youngsters of his own age will make all the difference to Socks," said Big Tom.

"Roughing it and learning to fend for himself will develop his character," added Little Tom.

The bears fidgeted and Hobson flicked his tail. They all thought of the cats' quarters in the sexton's lodge—the cat flap on the back door, the bowl marked *Pussy* always filled with the top of the milk, and their chair beside the stove where, after coming off duty, they would sleep all day with their black noses sunk deep in their furry flanks.

"After Socks's disappointment at the coal merchant's, when his hopes were raised so stupidly by those who should have known better, I think he deserves some fun," said Hobson, looking hard at the cats. "As for his character, I think that will do very well as it is."

Before Socks visited the yard again, Boots went through the Highway Code with him, paying particular attention to Part Two, which is intended for the road user on wheels.

"You're to do as Winks says," Boots told him. "There's to be no more riding with no hands, or dawdling about at the back of the trucks and darting out from behind." And Socks promised.

During the next few weeks Socks was happier than he had ever been. Every day someone picked him up and took him down to the yard. Sometimes it was Joshua on the tipper coal truck, or a young friend of

Winks on the ice-cream truck, but mostly it was Feathers on the mail truck.

Slippers and the small white bear were soon firm friends.

"It's a shame her fur is in such a state," Slippers told Boots. "It's the very best quality nylon. The next time the postman has circulars to deliver to all the houses in Station Road she's going to let me give it a good dry shampoo with talcum powder and I'm sure it will come up as good as new."

Feathers always took special care to bring Socks home at the time he was expected. Once, on a wet day when he grumbled because Slippers had insisted on his wearing an extra long mackintosh made from a flowered plastic sponge bag, Feathers had spoken quite sharply to him.

"You ought to be glad to have someone who bothers about you," she said. "I should be. Slippers being there and caring is what it means to have a real home. If she wasn't fond of you, she wouldn't fuss."

Afterward Socks gave her half a mothball and a scarf Audrey Trinket had knitted long ago in rainbow-colored wool.

One evening, Socks came home with an invitation for the other bears to visit the station yard.

"Winks says it won't be a real party but just a get-together so that you can meet them all," Socks explained. "He'll help with transport. A cable-drum truck will be passing this way about lunchtime. They're bound to slow up before taking the corner —nothing so large could do it without shifting gears. Winks says a brown velvet cat always rides on the back by the rear light, and if you're quick, she'll soon have you aboard."

"I'm sure we should both love to accept the invitation . . ." said Slippers.

"But though it's good of Winks to think of it, we'll arrange our own transport," Boots added hastily.

"You mean you'll come in that old doll's carriage?" said Socks without looking up.

"Naturally," said Boots. "Even if the back wheels do wobble, it's still quite satisfactory for short distances."

From his usual place in the hall Hannibal noticed the smaller bear's downcast face. He knew that Socks would have liked Slippers and Boots to meet his new friends in a vehicle more worthy of them.

"If it would be any help, I'll give you all a lift," Hannibal suggested. "Having been in road haulage myself in a small way, I'd be interested. When the bells on my saddlecloth have had a good rub with metal polish, they make a fair show, especially on a foggy afternoon."

In spite of what Winks had said about it not being

a real party, the bears saw as soon as they arrived at
the yard that he and the others had gone to a good
deal of trouble to entertain them properly.

"We thought we'd have tea in that horse-box trailer
which is waiting to be collected," Winks explained
after he had greeted them. "Being a trailer for only
one horse, it's a good deal less drafty than the bigger
vans."

"That pink rabbit called Plush did the refreshments," Socks whispered as Winks helped Boots guide Hannibal up a duckboard set before a narrow door at the side of the horse box. "Plush knew how it ought to be done, because she was once in a proper nursery, and Feathers and Upsidaisy helped collect what she needed."

The bears blinked as they stood inside the horse box and looked about them. The slatted floor was spread with pages from the color supplements of Sunday newspapers which Watchit had provided from his van. Three tomato boxes upturned on their short peglegs formed a long buffet table. Small crackers were set beside each place, and down the center of the table were sprigs of holly and mistletoe with sprays of spruce.

"Those were bits left on the greengrocer's truck after their first Christmas stock was delivered," Socks explained. "Joshua and I helped get them."

"Upsidaisy did the floral decorations," said Winks. "The lady she belonged to before coming on the trucks went to special classes and had quite a knack."

The tea table with the china gleaming in the light from twisted, scarlet Christmas-tree candles was far better than anything Slippers had managed at home. There was a square covered dish with violets on it for sardines, a jam pot with a plated lid and a crested spoon, a ham with a frilled paper cuff, a teapot with a crocheted cozy, red, orange, and lemon drinks in plastic glasses for the younger animals, who didn't care for tea, and sugar bowls filled with pink and mauve lumps.

"They're really bath salts," Socks whispered. "Some bags burst on the truck that delivers to the druggist; and those drinks are done with cellophane wrapping paper pushed into the glasses."

"Not having to bother about real food helped a lot," Plush explained when Slippers complimented her on the effect. "We're fortunately placed as regards china and glass. Winks's van delivers to most of the best toy shops and there are often breakages. He brings along anything that's thrown out. Another of us travels on a truck with confectionery and Christmas novelties. That's how we came by the snappers. They'd been sent out with no bangers inside."

"And none the worse for that, I'm sure," said Slippers, who knew that Socks never really cared for the noisy snappers.

Slippers sat by Winks at the head of the table. His roughly mended back leg wouldn't swivel, so he ate standing, which enabled him to keep an eye on the wants of all his guests. Winks was such a kind host that even in the horse box with the domed roof high above they felt at home.

"I shouldn't bother with those sugar tongs," he

45

advised Boots after the big bear had struggled with them for some time. "They're just for show. We always use our paws."

Boots sat between Plush and Upsidaisy. The pink rabbit listened to all his tales of the shoe shop, and Upsidaisy's china ringlets swung gracefully to her shoulders in the candlelight.

Socks sat with Feathers and some of the younger animals at the foot of the table. The red feather in Joshua's cap dipped into his teacup, and several of the younger animals blew bubbles down their lemonade straws, but nobody minded. Hannibal stood nearby, using the cap from a thermos flask as a cup, with a pink paper crown from one of the snappers perched on his head. Joshua from the tipper truck took to the big elephant at once.

"You're a one!" he said as Hannibal pretended to blow out the candles around the cake with his trunk. "You're a caution and no mistake!" And Hannibal let the small monkey sit aloft on his back, grinning down at all the company.

Even Watchit was cheerful and once laughed so heartily that all the stitches showed along the seams of his blue velvet chest. Slippers had brought him a light blue bow off a box of handkerchiefs, and Hannibal pleased him by remarking that Cambridge seemed to have excellent prospects for the next boat race in March.

After tea, Winks showed them around the trucks. Boots had spent some time studying commercial motor traders' advertisements, and he was ready with knowledgeable questions about payload capacity, rear overhang, and telescopic hydraulic tipping gear. Shortening his stride to suit that of the smaller animal, Boots listened to all Winks told him about the great, brightly painted vehicles and Dr. Rudolf Diesel, who had given his name to the diesel fuel from which most of them gained their power.

They lingered longest in Winks's large toy van.

"We can carry as much as twelve tons," he told them as they looked around the lofty boxlike interior of the Dodge, "but mostly the toys and sportsgear, though bulky, are fairly light."

"Some of the loads are worth hundreds of pounds," added Plush. "That's why there's a padlock on the sliding door at the back."

Winks let them all bounce on the foam-filled cushion of the passenger seat in the cab, and even Slippers was impressed by the dual heater and defroster, the fresh-air blowers, windshield wipers, and wind-tone horns.

When the time came to leave, all the animals gathered around to watch Slippers and Socks mount Hannibal's broad back. While they settled themselves on the saddlecloth, Winks drew Boots aside. Once or twice as the two animals talked they glanced at Socks, and Slippers guessed it was the small bear's future they were discussing so gravely.

At home that night, when Hannibal was asleep in the hall with the pink paper crown still on his bent head, and when Socks had gone happily to bed, Boots told Slippers all that Winks had said.

"Winks is the first to realize that traveling as a mascot on the trucks may be no more than a passing fancy to Socks," said Boots as they sat before the kitchen stove, "but he told me Socks has a flair for the work and is remarkably keen. Nothing will keep him off a vehicle, whatever its destination. A municipal garbage truck's just the same to Socks as the smartest light pick-up truck. Winks won't press him either way, but he told me if Socks does decide to take up the work, he'll see that he has a good start with reasonable prospects. And apparently, if Socks is really interested, Winks has promised to take him out on the Dodge, so that he can see how he's shaping up."

"And does Socks seem interested?" asked Slippers quietly.

"Winks says he's been badgering him to take him all the time," said Boots.

The two bears sat still in the darkened room just as they had sat on the night after Socks had first gone on the trucks. What had seemed then to be only an enthralling new pastime was now clearly something far more serious. Boots poked the fire with the brass-knobbed poker. A cinder fell into the ash pan and glowed in the powdered ash. Slippers's side was smudged with mud where she had slipped from a hub cap while exploring one of the trucks. For once she did not bother to brush it off. At her side, Boots went on talking as if he were thinking aloud.

"At his age it's natural he should want to launch out . . . They're as good a crowd as you could wish to find. Rough, of course, but never likely to leave a friend in the lurch . . . It's not as though we've been able to find anything to do all together. Nothing that's worthwhile, at least . . . This is a chance for Socks, and the work would be really important."

Slippers spoke at last. She looked tired, but her voice was firm.

"Since we've let Socks go so far, it would be wrong to hinder him now. He must be free to choose for himself."

Nonstop

THE INVITATION from Winks for Socks to ride on the Dodge was delivered by Joshua one ice-cold morning a week before Christmas. The tipper coal truck had brought a load of coke to the house next door and the monkey had to shout above the noise of the engine.

"Winks says it's a run taking special orders around the district and you'll be back for tea. Feathers will pick you up when her truck clears the mailbox after lunch."

Socks started to prepare for the trip before the coal truck was out of sight. He brushed his fur and tried on his longest scarf, which crossed over his chest and fastened behind with a safety pin.

"Socks's new friends have certainly smartened him up," Boots remarked to Slippers. "He's spent half the

50

morning brushing his fur with a nail brush and soap-
suds in the bathroom."

"Then I hope he's not damp," said Slippers. "You
can't be too careful in this cold weather."

She hurried in search of Socks and made him sit
in the airing cupboard till his fur was bone-dry and
wouldn't leave the faintest smudge when he pressed
against a looking glass. Hannibal, who liked to be
warm, offered to keep Socks company in the cup-

board. While they stood under the slatted shelves piled with sheets and pillowcases, Socks told Hannibal about his trip that afternoon.

"It's what I've wanted ever since I first saw Winks on the Dodge from the coal merchant's window," said Socks. "If Winks thinks I'm any good, he's promised to help me work properly on the trucks like Joshua and all the others."

Hannibal looked down at Socks as he perched on one of the stone hot-water bottles Mrs. Trinket always kept to warm the beds.

"It would be a rougher life than you've been accustomed to," he said doubtfully. "But after this expedition you'll be able to judge if it's likely to suit you or not."

"That's what Winks thought," said Socks.

"You're bound to be gone for longer than on most of your trips," said Hannibal, "so I should mention it to Slippers and Boots. They'll appreciate it if you ask."

"Of course I'm going to ask them," said Socks, sliding down the side of the bottle. "There's no need to fuss!"

Socks had really intended to do so. He was only waiting for the best moment so that there would be no likelihood of either bear saying no.

If Boots hadn't been so gloomy about the weather

at lunch, Socks would have asked then. But throughout the morning, while he polished the family's shoes, Boots had kept Polly's transistor radio tuned to the weather forecasts meant for ships at sea.

"Visibility's nil in the Bristol Channel," he reported, "and out in the Atlantic there's heavy snow which is coming this way. The weatherman said a heavy fall's expected, with some drifting."

Slippers shivered as sleet drummed against the window and a rising gale shook the television aerial.

"We're lucky not to have to go out," she said. "Nothing's worse than snow for lodging in your fur and soaking through your canvas."

And while Socks fidgeted, she recounted the story of a bear who had tumbled from a carriage into a curb full of snow at Bromley in Kent.

"She was a cousin of mother's, twice removed," said Slippers. "The nursemaid put her to sit on a radiator for days and days till her fur scorched ginger, but the damage had been done and trouble had set in."

"Mildew, no doubt?" asked Boots, who had heard the story twice before and knew what was expected of him.

"Right in her straw," said Slippers.

"That's snow all over," said Boots. "Why some folk go off to foreign parts simply to sport in it I can never understand."

"But that bear was restuffed, wasn't she?" Socks asked impatiently.

"At a considerable cost," said Slippers. "If she hadn't been a special favorite, the work might never have been done. As it was, the fur had to be patched. It meant she had to wear a kilt ever after, just to hide the seam."

"And all for the sake of one heedless outing," said Boots, "on a day such as this, when any sensible bear would stay by the fire."

Slippers was in her usual place on the sitting-room windowsill that afternoon, watching the first snowflakes eddy around the lampposts, when the mail truck stopped outside. As the postman cleared the mailbox, Slippers heard the front door swing open. A second later, Socks scurried down the steps and joined Feathers on the front bumper of the mail truck. The two young bears chattered excitedly to one another as Slippers watched the van speed down the street till it was out of sight in the falling snow.

"I do wish Socks hadn't gone off with Feathers like that," said Slippers, when she told Boots and Hannibal what she had seen. "On a day like this it's far too cold for him to dawdle about in that station yard."

"He won't be there for long today," said Hannibal. "Didn't Socks tell you? Feathers is taking him as far as the yard. Then he'll join Winks for a trip on the Dodge."

Slippers looked at Boots with dismay. Through the open door an icy gale scattered snowflakes over the linoleum.

"Once Winks asked Socks to go with him, nothing we could have said would have stopped him," said Boots. "We always knew it would happen sooner or later."

The other bear didn't answer. She stared out into the deserted street. Snowflakes landed on her nose and melted there. Boots touched her arm, but she brushed his paw aside. Seeing her face, he knew that words wouldn't help. Behind him in the hall, the wind jingled the bells on Hannibal's saddlecloth. He turned to meet the eyes of the old elephant and without a word both of them knew what they must do.

At the station, snow covered the loaded coal cars as if the coal had been dredged with icing sugar. It stung the faces of the truck drivers as they loaded their vehicles with Christmas goods in the station yard. In spite of the cold, everyone was cheerful.

Plush's big eight-wheeler truck was already loaded. As Socks and Feathers drove into the yard, they saw her ready in the brightly lit cab. It was freshly decorated with paper carnations in the plastic vase, a sprig of holly, and two glitter balls.

"Plush will be on the road right over Christmas," explained Feathers as Socks scrambled down from the mail truck. "That's why she's decorated early."

"Won't she mind being away at Christmas?" Socks asked.

"We take the rough with the smooth," said Feathers, "and she's used to the life."

"Of course," said Socks and, squaring his shoulders, he set off toward the Dodge, which stood outside the freight depot on the far side of the yard.

Winks was perched in the center of the hood just above the company's badge. He was secured to the radiator grille with a stout piece of string. Snow speckled his fur, but when he caught sight of Socks he hailed him cheerfully.

"Cracker has only one more crate of walk-and-talk dolls to load on now, and then we'll be off," he said. "You'd better hop up."

Now the moment Socks had so long awaited had arrived, he hesitated. Even crossing the yard, he had slipped twice and ended up crawling on all fours. Now snow and grit covered his paws and already they felt very cold.

The hood of the van towered above him like a cliff. To scale it and reach Winks on his perch seemed an impossibility. Socks glanced around for help. All the other mascots were busy with their own concerns. Plush looked thoughtfully down at her paws as the engine of the Leyland truck was warmed up. From the parcels truck, Upsidaisy stared straight ahead with

unblinking eyes. Joshua was nowhere in sight, and
Feathers sat on the bumper of the mail truck not even
looking in his direction. Socks knew he was on his
own.

"The Dodge is higher than I thought," he called
up to Winks through a stinging mist of fine snow.
"I'm afraid I don't see how I'll ever climb it."

"Course you don't, till I've told you," shouted
Winks. "It's easy as falling off a log, once you know

how. You'll find a foothold in the chassis behind the front wheel. Once you're on it, you'll be able to edge around to the front with handholds most of the way."

Socks found the domed foothold and balancing on an old gasoline can, he scrambled up. The surface of the van was slippery as ice. He did not dare look down as he edged his way along a ledge beside the passenger's door and crawled forward until he gained a hold on one of the headlights on the front of the van.

"That's first-rate!" said Winks as Socks clung to the light with both paws. "Now follow that ledge across to the grille and you'll have done it."

Socks released his hold on the light and moved on. Only a ridge on the chassis served as a handhold. The grille, where Winks awaited him, seemed yards away. Without meaning to do so, Socks looked down. Below, past the headlights and bumper with its towing rings, was only a frozen puddle, dark against the snow. Socks knew he was stuck. He didn't dare move forward or back. He was too frightened even to call out. As he clung to the chassis, with his eyes shut, Socks felt a small metal object whiz past his head and a line attached to it tangle around his arm.

"Hold on to my watering can and I'll soon have you across," said Winks. "It often comes in handy at first."

A second later, Socks was clutching the line and Winks was pulling him to safety.

"Now I'll fix you to the grille with this strap and you'll be safe as houses," said Winks. "We've telescopic shock absorbers, but with snow on the roads there are bound to be bumps, and it's silly to take chances."

Fastened to the bars of the grille with a much-chewed puppy's collar, Socks forgot his fears and was ready to enjoy the ride.

"This won't be much more than a spin," Winks explained as the van swung out of the yard, "but I thought it would give you the feel of it. The load we have aboard is really expensive toys which have been ordered specially. I shouldn't like to guess what the whole lot's worth. The model cars alone would run into hundreds, and there's a doll house that costs more than some folk would spend on a garage."

Socks waved as the van passed his own home in Station Road. To his surprise, not even Slippers was in her usual place behind the lace curtains on the sitting-room windowsill, and his greeting went unanswered.

Socks was too excited to be disappointed for long. In the High Street, colored lights were looped above the thoroughfare, and Christmas trees shone through the falling snow. The driver halted twice to deliver goods, then he swung his van out of the shopping area and they drove more swiftly down a tree-lined road.

"Most of our toys are for a shop right outside the town on the new housing estate," Winks explained. "It'll give you a chance to see how the van travels once she's on the open road."

Soon the town was behind them. The road was deserted. The light was fading and the snowflakes whirled more thickly in the beams of the headlights.

Rounding a bend, they saw a car parked at the side of the road. Two men muffled in sheepskin jackets and scarves bent over the open hood. As the Dodge came in sight, one of the men signaled the driver to stop.

"It must be a breakdown," said Winks as the driver halted the van on the shoulder and trudged back down the road. "Cracker wouldn't leave anyone stranded. If he can't get them moving again, he'll take a message on to the nearest garage."

With the engine silent behind them, nothing stirred. The fields on either side were shrouded with snow. It coated the bumper below them and the curved windshield above their heads. On the parked van, Socks suddenly felt uneasy. His home in Slumber Lightly seemed very far away. Without their driver, he knew that even on the van with all its wonders he and Winks were powerless. He looked at Winks to see if he shared his feeling of panic, but the small rabbit seemed unmoved.

"Don't you think Cracker's being rather a long time?" Socks asked, but even as he spoke they heard muffled voices and footsteps approaching the van.

"That must be Cracker now," said Winks, "and he's brought along one of those men. Probably he'll drop him off at the garage to guide the tow truck back to the car."

A minute later, the cab doors were slammed and the van moved forward.

"Cracker must be making up time," said Winks as they sped along far more rapidly than before. "He'll aim to finish his round before this snow gets any worse."

At his side, Socks held on grimly. Snow stung his eyes, and sand and flints from the gritted road cut at his sides like a thousand darts. The darkened countryside was no more than a blur as it flashed past. Once, beside an isolated cottage, Socks saw a row of gasoline pumps and a garage workshop, but to his surprise the van never slackened its speed.

"Cracker must have decided to drop his passenger at the next garage on the housing estate," explained Winks. "It's near the toy shop we're heading for, and that will save him stopping twice."

They saw the first rows of newly built houses a few minutes later.

"That's the shop where we drop the rest of our

stock," said Winks as they came to the shopping
center, "and the garage is next door. You can see their
pickup truck by the pumps."

Socks saw the toy shop ahead of them. Flaxen-
haired dolls smiled from their long cardboard boxes.
Giant teddy bears and golliwogs stood ready for their
first homes. The shop, glowing out of the darkness,
seemed as welcome to Socks as a safe anchorage after
a stormy voyage. Only the Dodge didn't stop. It
thundered past the toy shop, past the garage, past the
last familiar chain store and the last house with a
Christmas tree in the uncurtained picture window.
Ahead of them was only the darkened road across the
open moorland, where snow drove in blinding clouds
around them.

"Why didn't Cracker stop?" Socks shouted above the roar of the engine.

The rising blizzard scattered his companion's reply like chaff tossed into the wind. Winks cupped his paws over his mouth and shouted into the bear's ear.

"Cracker didn't stop because he's not at the wheel. Going at this speed isn't his style at all."

Socks twisted around to stare at Winks. The rabbit's ears were pricked in the glow from the headlights and his voice was steady.

"Back there, when those men stopped Cracker to help with their car, it must have been a holdup! They've stolen the van with everything in it and one of them is driving us now."

Socks was scared. His paws felt like blocks of ice. The snow had lodged in the folds of his muffler. When it melted, he would be soaked through to his straw. Like Slippers's mother's cousin twice removed, he thought, and then stopped himself because he didn't want to think of Slippers or Boots just then.

"Where do you suppose they're taking us?" he asked.

"To a town on the coast most likely," said Winks, "though with a driver like this I doubt if we'll ever get there. I've never known anyone to make such a hash of the gears."

Socks was silent. He hesitated to ask a further question, yet he knew it would be better to face the truth.

"Where do you think Cracker is?" he asked at last.

"Knocked out near that car and dumped in the ditch," said Winks shortly. "He wouldn't have let them take the truck's keys without a fight."

Winks said no more, and Socks knew how he must feel. Together they stared ahead of them into the darkness. Once, in a narrow lane, the branch of a hazel bent low by the snow whipped across the headlights and they heard the crack of glass, but still the van went on its course.

"I'm sorry your first trip on the Dodge should have turned out like this," said Winks after a long silence. "You mustn't let it put you off."

"Of course not," said Socks.

The van traveled faster and faster. Even in the darkness, they knew they were traveling downhill. The headlights shone on a road sign ordering motorists to shift to low gear for the next half mile. "That means the hill must be extra steep," said Winks, but the van never slackened its speed. On a sharp bend, when the driver at last tried to brake, the van skidded.

"Hold tight, we're off the road!" shouted Winks as branches splintered before them and the van came to rest in a snowdrift on the far side of a hedge.

For a moment after the crash, there was silence. The headlights glowed through the snow, which was piled against them. Socks blinked as he stared up at

the moon sailing swiftly through the clouds. The strap which had secured him to the grille had snapped. He lay well clear of the van on a fold of snow sprinkled with berries and leaves from the broken holly hedge. The van was tilted to one side, but the drift had saved it from turning over, and astride the long arm of the driver's rear-view mirror sat Winks.

"Just listen to those men in the cab," he whispered as Socks joined him. "They've been going at it hammer and tongs. The passenger told the driver he wasn't fit to be trusted with a kiddie car, and the driver said the smash was all the passenger's fault for not spotting that warning."

Both men looked white-faced and angry as they scrambled from the cab. After a brief inspection of the van and its load, they left it stranded in the snow-drift and trudged off down the road.

"That's the last of them for now," said Winks as their angry voices faded into the darkness, "but with stuff as valuable as this, they won't give up. Those men will be back as soon as they've found a truck or a Land-Rover with a four-wheel drive to winch the van back on the road, and before they come we must decide what to do."

As he spoke, Socks stiffened beside him.

"There's someone else in the back of the van," he whispered. "I heard the sliding door rattle as if someone was trying to push it up. Those men must have left it unpadlocked."

Together they made their way around to the rear of the van. As they waited in the moonlight, the sliding door opened, and through the narrow space wriggled Slippers and Boots.

Danger Ahead

"SLIPPERS AND I thought we'd come for the ride," Boots explained. "We slipped aboard with the last of those walk-and-talk dolls."

"Not that we thought you wouldn't take good care of Socks," Slippers assured Winks. "I only felt if anything did go wrong I would rather be near than at home worrying."

Winks was silent. He knew a good deal had gone wrong and that but for him Socks would still be safe with the other bears in their comfortable home.

"Hannibal told us where Socks had gone," Boots explained. "He's in the van as well, with his head wedged in the front porch of that doll house."

"One of the walk-and-talk dolls is right on top of him," added Slippers. "She keeps on calling him Ma-

ma and reciting a nursery rhyme. It's annoying him a good deal."

Winks and Socks told the bears all that had happened, while they set about freeing Hannibal. Winks and Socks entered the large doll house through the double garage and pushed the wedged elephant from the front while the others pulled from the rear.

"Boots was sure something was amiss because of the way the van was traveling," said Slippers rather breathlessly as they all tugged and pushed, "though neither of us dreamed of a holdup!"

"And that we had been hijacked," added Boots, who had always wanted to use the word and never imagined he would have the chance to do so.

With a final heave, Hannibal was freed. Winks switched off the talking doll before she recited *Little Bo-Peep* still another time, and replaced her in the crate with the other dolls. While Slippers thumped the worst of the snow off everyone's fur, they considered their position.

"Winks is sure those thieves will come back," said Socks, "as soon as they've found another truck or a Land-Rover to tow the Dodge back on the road. When we heard you, we were trying to decide what we ought to do when they arrive."

Boots frowned as they huddled together on the tilted floor of the stranded van.

"It's hard to see what good any of us could do here when they do come," he said. "If Hannibal's agreeable, I really think our most sensible course is to make our own way home."

He looked toward Hannibal, who stared from the back of the van at the drifts of snow and the rough track the van had carved through the holly hedge. His forehead was streaked with paint from the porch of the doll house, and one of his wheels was chipped.

"I'll do my best," Hannibal said, "though it won't be as smooth a ride as you'd have with a six-cylinder diesel engine and a five-speed gearshift. After the Dodge, you're bound to notice a vast difference. We'll arrive some time—when is another matter."

As the bears hesitated, Winks spoke.

"You must all do as you think best, but I'll have to stay. You see, now that Cracker's gone, I'm responsible for the van."

Winks stood at the entrance to the van under the sliding door. With the van towering dark above, he looked smaller than ever. The moonlight shone on the watering can slung from his shoulder, and his head was erect. Even his fur smelled of packing boxes and diesel oil.

Boots spoke before Socks could stop him.

"We know how you must feel, and it does you credit, but what on earth would you be able to do?"

Winks wasn't offended.

"You're new to road haulage, and it's not to be expected you'd guess, but so long as I'm aboard, the van will be that much easier for the police to trace. Those thieves will change the license plates and give the van a paint job, but with any luck they won't notice me up on the hood. Cracker's bound to mention me when he has his say to the police, and they'll be on the lookout, you can be sure of that! Much the same thing happened with Plush on her Leyland, and the men who took it were caught red-handed before they were off the highway."

There was silence as Winks stopped speaking. Socks stood close at his side with his eyes on Boots. Slippers knew as they waited that what Boots decided now was more important to Socks than any decision the older bear had ever made.

"Naturally, if you're staying, we shall too," said Boots. "None of us knows the ropes, so you must tell us what to do, and I hope we shall be some help at least."

After the decision was made, Winks took charge. Although he was the smallest, he knew his way about the large vehicle so well that it seemed natural to them all to do as he suggested.

"While we wait for someone to turn up, we might as well make ourselves as comfortable as possible,"

Winks decided. "Cracker and I have spent a night on the van more than once, and it shouldn't be too uncomfortable."

They pulled down the sliding door to keep out the cold. Slippers and Boots settled themselves in a large doll carriage with a double hood. Hannibal stood nearby between the crates of walk-and-talk dolls and a portable wading pool, and Socks and Winks shared the front seat of a red model sports car.

Once they were settled, there was more time to think. Slippers noticed Winks hadn't said who he thought most likely to reach them first—the two thieves or the police.

"Even if we're lucky and it is the police," she whispered to Boots, "it will be all right for Winks, but how will they know who the rest of us are and where we belong?"

"Once we're missed at home, the Trinkets will be sure to trace us," said Boots. "The police would be the first people they'd ask."

Slippers said no more. She was doubtful that anyone in the busy house at Station Road would notice their absence for some days at least. Bill and Simon were hard at work at the choir school practicing Christmas carols, and Audrey had not yet started her holidays. In the old days, Polly Trinket would have been the first to miss them, but lately she had seemed interested only in the young salesman from the shoe factory and when they would have enough money saved up to be married.

Not even the danger they were all in spoiled Socks's pleasure in sitting in the sports car. It had lights which really worked and a horn that sounded on three different notes. When Socks finally fell asleep with his paws on the steering wheel, he dreamed that he and Winks were competing for their country in the Monte Carlo Rally. They were well ahead, roaring down the road toward the sunlit Mediterranean town, when Socks woke up.

The hum of the engine which he had heard in his dream was real enough, but it came from the van as they sped once more along the dark road. There was no sign of Winks at his side.

"We're moving again!" Socks told the other bears when he finally reached them. "Those thieves must have come back when we were all asleep and towed the van back on the road."

Boots sat up with a jerk and banged his head on the hood of the doll carriage. Beside him, Slippers kept tight hold on the sides of the carriage, which rocked as they sped along.

"Where's Winks?" Boots asked. "Does he know what's happened?"

"Winks climbed back on the hood when those men

arrived with a mechanic and a pickup truck," said Hannibal calmly from his enclosure by the wading pool. "He didn't want to wake you, but it seemed certain they would get the van on its way and he wanted to be ready. He said that once we were on the road again, we were all to stay put and he'd try to look in at the next stop."

The bears huddled around Hannibal as the van carried them through the still darkened countryside. Once they heard the cry of gulls and the sound of waves breaking against the rocks far below. They knew they must have reached the coast, just as Winks had expected. Soon they descended a steep hill into what they thought must be a busy coastal town.

"This is where the police may spot us," said Boots, but the van swung out of the stream of traffic into a narrow alley. A moment later, it stopped. Heavy doors of what they guessed to be a warehouse were pushed open and the Dodge was driven inside.

The bears and Hannibal, hidden behind the crates of dolls, hardly dared to breath as one of the men jumped down from the driving cab, walked around to the rear of the van, and pushing up the sliding door, peered inside.

"Everything's pretty shipshape in here, Joe," he reported to the driver.

"Better padlock it for now, then," the driver suggested. "We don't want any of this little lot pinched before it's shipped. The skipper says there's not a chance of sailing now till the next high tide tonight and we daren't risk loading till dusk." When the bears and Hannibal heard the sliding door rolled down and the padlock snap into place, they knew they were imprisoned and that before nightfall they would be on the high seas.

As they huddled together in the darkened van, a ventilator in the roof snapped open and Winks stared down at them through the small opening.

"All right inside there?" he asked. "Joshua and I often come up here for a bit of a scramble. There's a stud or two for a handhold when you come to the overhang but I don't think you'd better try it."

"Of course we shan't," Boots told him shortly as Socks eagerly looked up at the ventilator, "and we're not all right. Those men padlocked the van, so we're prisoners."

"And by tonight we'll be on the high seas in a ship going anywhere," added Socks.

"No one in Slumber Lightly will even know what's happened," added Slippers. "We didn't even have a chance to say goodbye."

"The people at home know a good deal about the stolen van already," said Winks cheerfully, "and after what I told Flyover at the traffic light they should know considerably more pretty soon."

The bears stared up at Winks. The light had

brightened and they could see him sitting by the ventilator with his legs trailing over the edge of the small opening. Boots growled. The names of Winks's friends always muddled him, and coming upon another at such a time was too much even for his good temper. Hannibal touched Boots's arm gently with his trunk before he could growl again, and Slippers stepped into the breach with her usual good manners.

"Flyover," she repeated, "now let me see, I don't think we've had the pleasure of meeting her, have we?"

"Probably you haven't," said Winks. "Flyover was once a fairy on a Christmas tree. Now she rides on a gasoline-tank truck that serves most of the garages hereabouts. The Dodge pulled up alongside her truck just as we came into Cliffport this morning and we had time for a chat. Flyover told me there's a first-rate hue and cry. The Dodge's picture is in all the papers and there's lots about Cracker. Flyover said he's in the hospital with a nasty bump on the head, but it would take more than that to stop him helping the police all he can."

"However did Flyover know so much?" asked Socks.

"Watchit saw all about the holdup in the newspapers on his truck," replied Winks, "and the news was all over the country in no time. Flyover picked

it up from Tallyho. His telephone-repair truck was mending a line the snow brought down on the other side of the town. Flyover's truck is based here, but Slumber Lightly's not thirty miles away, so we've friends in common, and she takes an interest."

Boots shifted his paws impatiently.

"But how will meeting her help us?" he asked. "There's not a lot of time."

"I'm coming to that," said Winks. "The gasoline truck was off to a garage in Slumber Lightly this morning, and Flyover promised to take a message about our whereabouts. It's that garage near the movie house and they don't sell diesel oil, so none of the trucks is likely to be in, but she's bound to see someone, even if it's only one of the cats."

"There is Bret," said Socks eagerly. "He's always at the garage on the workshop bench near the foreman's cap and the lunch boxes."

Boots glanced at Slippers.

"Socks means that long-haired young tabby who's always asleep on the oily rags. Bret is Big Tom's nephew, though he's such a loafer he never mentions him. I doubt if we can put much trust in him."

"But Hobson's often said if Bret would only smarten himself up he'd be bright enough," said Slippers hopefully.

"And Bret would know exactly what to do in an

78

adventure," added Socks. "Every evening he watches cowboy films on television in the manager's apartment upstairs. However late they last, Bret always watches to the end. That's why he's so sleepy in the daytime."

Even Winks was thoughtful as he left the bears and took up his position on the hood of the van. Although help might come as he had hoped, he knew they would be wise to have a plan ready so that when the time came they would be able to help themselves.

The others waited inside the van. All through the day they listened to the sounds which came from the docks near the warehouse where they were imprisoned and to the call of a foghorn far out to sea. They knew their hope of rescue rested on the grubby fairy doll perched on the gasoline truck now speeding toward Slumber Lightly, and on Bret, who seemed most likely to be the only person on hand to receive her message. Thinking of the shaggy young cat, who had never bestirred himself enough to scare even a mouse away from the remains of a cheese sandwich, even Slippers and Socks were forced to agree with Boots that their chance of rescue was slight.

Bret Bestirs Himself

BRET, THE young half-Persian cat at the garage in Slumber Lightly, was bored. If he left the swept front court to roam among the abandoned cars and piles of discarded tires on the empty lot next door, globs of snow gathered on his shaggy fur and he couldn't be bothered to lick them off. When Bret returned to the warmth of the workshop, the globs melted into his bed of oily rags and he was forced to find a new resting place on the foreman's cap. All that week business had been slack. Few motorists had ventured out. The sale of Christmas stockings filled with car sponges and wax polish hadn't been brisk.

The night before, a power failure had spoiled Bret's favorite television program. Fluffy, the elderly cat who lived at the nearby movie house, had sent him packing when he tried to enter the theater through a cloakroom window during the second half of a cowboy epic. Flicking his ear, Bret had set off for the parish hall to watch a missionary film about Dr. Livingstone. The Bishop, who had arrived in the vestibule at the same time, would have let Bret in out of the cold if Big Tom hadn't bustled up and hustled Bret away as he rubbed his bullet head against the Bishop's buttoned gaiters.

When the gasoline truck pulled in at the garage that morning, Bret would have welcomed any excitement. He listened eagerly to all Flyover told him about the missing van and the plight of its occupants.

"Winks wants everyone here to know he and the bears and Hannibal are with the van near the docks at Cliffport," the fairy doll told Bret. "Winks couldn't be sure, but he thought that was where the thieves were headed. He said he'll do what he can, but he'll need all the help you can muster. If it doesn't come before nightfall, he thinks it might be all over for them. They'll be shipped on the high tide."

No one had ever depended on Bret before. In all Slumber Lightly only Hobson at the grocer's, and the Bishop when he stopped at the garage for gas, ever had a good word for him. Now, as the gasoline truck rolled on its way and Flyover grinned at him from the bumper, Bret's heart was full of pride. He felt like the hero in one of his favorite cowboy stories. Thundering hooves rang in his ears as Bret raced through the town, up alleyways, over garden walls, across snow-covered lawns, and in and out of houses and shops. At every point Bret paused only long enough to deliver Winks's rallying call, then he was gone. Everywhere he was met with generous offers

of help, from the smallest mascot on a tradesman's truck, to the oldest of the bears' friends among the cats of Slumber Lightly.

"You can bank on us," Big Tom told Bret, with all his disapproval of the young tabby forgotten.

"Up to the hilt!" said Little Tom as they abandoned their watch on a mousehole behind the postcard and guide-book counter in the cathedral.

"Of course we must think of something," said Hobson, when Bret found the big black and white cat in the grocer's in Cordwainer's Row. "It would never do for the bears and Hannibal to leave the country. A day trip to Calais or even a well-conducted coach tour to the capitals of Europe is one thing, but for them to be sent away forever would be out of the question. Socks and Winks might manage, but the others would never be able to settle down."

Seated on his usual chair by the bacon counter, Hobson thought about the problem while Bret padded up and down outside, not even glancing at the display of tangerines, candied fruit, plum puddings, and Christmas cakes in the shop window.

After a while, Hobson rose and paid a brief visit to Polly Trinket's shoe shop next door. Looking rather more cheerful, he joined Bret on the pavement a few minutes later and dispatched him on several errands.

That afternoon Cordwainer's Row was deserted. The shops were shut because it was Wednesday and early closing day in the city. Not a cat was in sight, but the freshly fallen snow on the sidewalk was patterned with many paw marks.

Outside the shoe shop stood Polly Trinket's fiancé's small green delivery truck. That afternoon the young shoe salesman had pocket diaries to deliver to all the shops in the surrounding towns which stocked his company's footwear. Since it was her half day, Polly was going with him for the ride. They had parked the loaded truck in Cordwainer's Row while they lunched in the town before setting out on their trip. At the last minute Polly, thinking of the snowy journey ahead, asked Frank to wait on the corner of Station Road while she ran home to change into warmer clothes.

"Sorry I've been so long," Polly said when she joined him, "but Audrey's school closed early today because of the snow. She was at home all alone and a bit upset. Just for company, till mother comes back from her job at the café, she thought she'd play with Hannibal and the bears, but she couldn't find one of them."

Frank smiled at Polly's flushed face as she hurried back to the truck with him.

"And did you find them for her?" he asked.

"I tried," said Polly with a frown. "We turned out every drawer and cupboard, but there wasn't a sign of them. Audrey will be all right because I've sent her along to the café, but it really is a puzzle. I searched high and low, and in such a small house there's nowhere they could be."

The small green truck contained far more than the neatly labeled pocket diaries Frank had left there at lunchtime, with a special order of snowboots and several boxes of samples. In the darkest corner of the truck, Hobson and Bret curled behind a pile of shoe boxes. With paws folded under their narrow chests, Big Tom and Little Tom crouched under the front seats. Under the dashboard, hidden behind the Footwear Retailer's Manual and the A.A. Handbook, sat Watchit, and on the front bumper, sheltered by a bunch of dried heather, were Joshua and Feathers.

A great many more of the town cats and Winks's friends had volunteered to come, but there had been no more space. As it was, Hobson found such a mixed rescue party hard to handle. They had been hidden in the truck since lunch. Waiting for so long in the cramped quarters made everyone touchy and on edge.

Hobson knew the plans he had improvised so quickly were likely to be as full of leaks as a plastic bucket after being filled with hot cinders. A lot would depend on luck and on how much Winks and the others might be able to do to help themselves. From all he knew of Winks, Hobson guessed that the small rabbit would never surrender easily, although he realized the odds that were against them, and was uneasy. Normally during the lunch hour Hobson took a nap in a warm corner of the shop beside a sack of coffee beans, but today his companions made even the shortest forty winks impossible by constantly asking questions.

"Even if there is a pocket diary and that special order of snowboots for the shoe shop in Cliffport on board, are you sure Frank will deliver them today?"

"And in such a large town, will we ever find Boots and the others?"

"And supposing we do, how will we be able to help them?"

Joshua and Feathers also passed back their questions and suggestions through Watchit. The wires under the dashboard acted like a telephone and he was usually able to catch what they said.

"Feathers says wouldn't it be quicker to travel on one of the post-office parcel trucks? There's bound to be something going that way from the central sorting office."

"Joshua thinks we might have done better at the bus depot. Quite a few buses are still running."

"Feathers and Joshua are fed up with waiting!

They want to go on ahead. They'll hop on anything that seems likely, down at the traffic light."

Only the garage cat was no trouble. He was surprisingly helpful.

"Of course we must keep together," he insisted. "No one's going off on some harebrained scheme of their own. A rescue party's not a party at all if you split up. Hobson knows best. He heard Frank tell Polly, when he was in the shop this morning, that they would have to go all the way to Cliffport with those boots. Frank had gone in specially to make sure it would be all right."

Even Hobson knew that the garage cat had left most of the questions unanswered. Exactly how they would find the bears and Winks in the strange town, or what they would be able to do if they were lucky enough to discover them before it was too late, was no clearer to Hobson than it was to the others in his party. All the old cat knew was that Winks and the bears and Hannibal were in peril. Somehow they must be found, and no risk was too great to take if it would save them.

The Nick of Time

THE DELIVERY truck bowled along with all its passengers. On the front bumper Feathers and Joshua were hidden in the mist. Frank Fielding was too busy driving along the snow-packed country roads to notice an occasional mew or rustle. Polly Trinket was still worried about the missing toys. She was sure they weren't in the house. Long ago she and Frank had planned the part the bears and Hannibal would play in their future life together. However difficult it might be to wait and save until they had enough money to marry, the bears and Hannibal's being there had made all the difference. They were a part of her future which already existed, and they made all the rest seem more possible.

"Your mother would never have given the bears

and Hannibal away without asking," said Frank. "They're bound to turn up, unless whoever took that toy van yesterday stole them as well."

Polly smiled.

"Of course no one would. The bears aren't worth anything, except to us."

Frank frowned as he followed the road across the moor. He wished he could afford to marry Polly and provide her at once with all she longed for, without waiting and being sensible. Polly had had to be sensible for so long, he thought, ever since her father had died and she had gone to work in the shoe shop straight from school.

Delivering the diaries to shops in several different towns and villages took a long time. It was dark when they finally drove down the hill into Cliffport. The tide was almost full. Waves slammed against the sea wall and spray fell like hail on the roof of the van. In the harbor a cargo ship rode at anchor with her lights lit and smoke already blowing from her funnels.

"It's a rotten night for anyone to go to sea," said Frank, "but it looks as if that ship will be weighing anchor soon."

As they drove through the town past the brightly lit shops, Polly was puzzled. The van seemed full of muffled noises. Once, as she looked out of the side window, she felt something brush against her cheek like the feathered tip of a cat's ear, yet when she swung around there was nothing to be seen.

"The shop we want is in the High Street," said Frank, "but with so much traffic about I'll have to park down a side street at the back. There's a trade entrance behind the shop and if I go in that way I won't have to keep you waiting for long."

Frank swung the van down a narrow alleyway beside the shoe shop and came to a stop in a dimly lit street flanked by high warehouse walls. With the package of snowboots under his arm, he hurried off into the darkness.

Alone in the parked truck, Polly shivered. The street was deserted. In the distance she heard the sound of a foghorn far out to sea. There was the smell of seaweed and salt-soaked wharves. She knew they must be near the docks.

Behind her, the noises she thought she had imagined before began again. Only now they were louder. A shoe box tumbled over and dark shapes moved. When she twisted around to look, eyes glowed at her from the darkness. Polly thought of the toy van which had been stolen the day before and sprang out of the truck. With her flashlight in her hand, she darted around to the back and flung open the doors.

In the flashlight's beam stood the big black and white cat from the grocer's shop in Cordwainer's

Row. Several empty shoe boxes lay tumbled around him and his bushy tail moved restlessly over his arched back.

"Why, it's Hobson," said Polly with a smile. "You must have come all this way asleep in the back."

She put out her hand to stroke him, but as she did so, the big cat leaped from the truck and bolted away from her, down the darkened street.

Polly raced after him, while the other cats streamed

through the open doors of the van, traveling less swiftly because of Feathers, Joshua, and Watchit, whom they carried in their mouths.

Hobson's eyes flashed in the dark. He knew Polly Trinket was close at his heels and that the others would be coming up behind. Somehow he must keep ahead and lead them to the bears. He doubled down street after street, with the sound of lapping water growing louder in his ears.

Polly saw the dark shape of the van parked on the side of the wharf as she came out of an alley onto the dockside. Across the water in the harbor, the lighted cargo ship still rested at anchor. At the rear of the large van, two men were unloading goods into a rowboat moored to the wharf. As Polly looked up and down for the lost cat, an angry voice from the rowboat attracted her attention.

"Hey, Joe, I'm not taking these! They'd never pass for new! As old as the hills I'd say they were, and not worth the cargo space."

There was a hasty consultation between the two men by the van.

"The rest of the stuff's good enough. Joe says if you don't want that lot, just pitch it over the side. Those old bears will sink soon enough."

The words chilled Polly's heart, and forgetting everything else, she ran forward. Shining her light into the rowboat, she saw Boots and Slippers and

Socks lying in the bottom and Hannibal already poised on the gunwale, ready to be tipped into the water.

"Don't you dare drop Hannibal in," Polly shouted to the sailor who was holding him. "Those bears and that toy elephant belong to my brothers and sister. I don't know how you got hold of them, but I want them back."

The two men by the van swung around. As the sailor stared up at Polly, his face turned pale and Hannibal slipped from his grip. For a second Hannibal's stand wobbled on the gunwale balanced over the water, then a wave lifted the boat and he toppled back onto the bears.

"Now we don't want no unpleasantness nor harsh words," said the sailor as he gathered up the toys and thrust them into Polly's arms. "If these belong to your little brothers and sister, you're welcome to take them away, but how they got in with the rest of the toys is a mystery, for it's an export order straight from the factory and we've top priority to ship it tonight."

"Not till the police have seen if those are the stolen goods," said a voice, and swinging around, Polly saw Frank at her side. "And I fancy they are, because that van's the Dodge which was stolen yesterday. I'd have known it anywhere on account of that toy rabbit up on the front."

For a second there was silence as Frank and Polly faced the men on the deserted wharf. Then Hobson bounded forward, followed by the other cats. And from inside the van, so that all the town should hear, the horns of all the model sports cars sounded, and all the walk-and-talk dolls recited *Little Bo-Peep has lost her sheep,* at the tops of their shrill voices.

Safe and Sound

SUPPER IN the Trinkets' house took a long time that night. Mrs. Trinket brewed tea and made it extra sweet with condensed milk. She fried every rasher of bacon they had in the larder, with eggs and baked beans and sausages meant for the next day's lunch. The bears and Hannibal steamed before the kitchen stove with Polly's hooded jacket and mittens. Frank and Polly sat side by side, and Bill and Simon and Audrey never stopped plying them with questions.

"Tell us again about the cats," begged Audrey, "and how Hobson led you right to our bears and Hannibal and the stolen van."

"Hobson must have been asleep in Frank's delivery truck when we started," explained Polly. "I've known him to jump into a truck parked near his shop before.

Once he went right up to London in a fancy-cakes truck and had to be sent back with the next delivery of Swiss rolls."

"But who were all the other cats?" asked her younger brother.

"That we'll never know for sure," Frank told him.

"The police thought they must have been stray cats who often hang about the docks."

"But the one who jumped right on the man in the boat did look just like that scruffy tabby down at the garage," said Polly.

"And there were two black cats who were the living image of Big Tom and Little Tom in the cathedral," added Frank.

Bill and Simon stared.

"That tabby wasn't in the garage when I went for a flashlight battery this afternoon," said Bill.

"And Big Tom and Little Tom weren't in the cathedral after lunch," added Simon. "When we were practicing *Oh, little town* . . . I noticed especially."

Mrs. Trinket smiled as she refilled the teapot.

"I've never heard such nonsense as you're all imagining. Hobson bolting from Frank's delivery truck in a strange town and chancing upon that stolen toy van's one thing, but a whole troop of cats arriving from Slumber Lightly's quite another. What puzzles me is how your bears and Hannibal came to be on that toy van at all. Nothing else is missing from the house, and no burglars in their right senses would have dreamed of taking them."

But no one was able to explain the mystery.

Later that evening, when Frank had gone home and the family were in bed, Boots and Hannibal decided to go out once more into the town in search of news about their friends.

"Hobson's bound to know something because he came home later than us in that police car with the driver who was the nephew of the manager of his grocer's shop," Boots told Slippers as she helped him into a pair of old boots and a cape made from part of a plastic curtain which had once hung in the bathroom. "We shan't rest easy till we know everyone's safe."

Left alone in a basket chair by the fire, Slippers let Socks talk about all their adventures until he was almost asleep.

"Wasn't it clever of Winks to switch on the walk-and-talk dolls and use the car horns as a signal to the police? He saved his plan till the very last minute, like soldiers not firing till they see the whites of the enemy's eyes. That police sergeant who came in the first patrol car said he'd never heard such a hullabaloo, and he told Frank those thieves would probably be sent to prison for three years."

"Or more!" said Slippers, remembering the Dodge's driver, who would spend his Christmas with a sore head in the hospital.

The cathedral clock had chimed midnight when Boots wheeled Hannibal into the washhouse. As Boots stood in the kitchen doorway, stamping the worst of the snow from his Wellingtons, the others knew from his face that all was well.

"I've seen Hobson and everyone's accounted for," he said. "Big Tom and Little Tom are back in the sexton's lodge, and Bret's at the garage. He was in ample time to watch the main feature film on the manager's television."

"However did they come home so quickly?" asked Slippers.

"In the trunk of the police inspector's car," replied the big bear. "Bret gave them the tip. He knew it would come this way, and Divisional Headquarters is handy to the center of town. Hannibal and I just looked in to thank Bret for all he's done. He was civil, of course, but he barely took his eyes off the screen. Bret has gone over to detective plays now, and Hobson thinks that, as he seems interested, there might be an opening for him with the police. They've their own canteen at the station, and with cheese sandwiches on sale, and currant buns, you can't be too careful about mice."

"And what happened to Winks and the rest?" Socks asked anxiously. "None of them came back with us on the van."

Boots warmed his paws before the fire so that the pads steamed.

"Hobson did what he could to keep an eye on them, though it wasn't easy to keep track. They were here, there, and everywhere, and so accustomed to fending for themselves that he could see they didn't welcome any interference. Hobson said Winks and the rest could all have come back on the squad car. Big Tom and Little Tom and Bret were all standing by to lift them up on the bumper, but none of them would go. They wanted to watch till the very last moment when the thieves were taken off in a patrol wagon. Winks and Joshua and Watchit were up on the roof of the Dodge most of the time, to have a better view. Feathers would have joined them, only her white ribbon tangled in the windshield wipers and she was stuck halfway."

"Did someone help her?" Socks interrupted anxiously.

"Winks saw to it," said Boots. "They take good care of one another, I must say, even if they won't stand fussing from others. Hobson said it gave him a chance for a word with Winks about getting them all home, though he might have saved his breath.

100

'Now we're in Cliffport, we might as well make a night of it!' Winks told him. 'It's not often we have a chance of a get-together.' Seemingly, there's a transport café near the docks and they meant to make off to it and pass the time of day with any mascots pulled up outside on the long-distance trucks. Afterwards they planned to move on to the coast road, where dozens of trucks are snowbound on the hill. Winks said there was nothing like a good traffic holdup for meeting folks they hadn't seen for years. He fancied his Aunt Antifreeze might show up from the Midlands, and Two Hoots and Howsthat from Scotland. A rough, tough lot they sounded like, I must say. Winks expected it would be dawn before most of the heavy vehicles got away, and he and the others meant to make an all-night party of it."

"But what will happen if it snows any more?" Slippers asked with a shiver.

"Bless you—that's what Winks wanted!" said Boots. "He told Hobson that with a good fleet of snowplows and blowers to clear the drifts, and sand trucks following on, they'd be sure of a lift home by breakfast."

"Well, I'm thankful Socks was sensible and came back with us," said Slippers. "He's tired enough as it is."

In the basket chair, Socks was silent. He thought

101

longingly of Winks and all his other friends gathered in the glow of a truck's rear light, with snow falling around them and the stars above.

"There was a message Winks wanted passed on to Socks," Boots added. "It was to say they were all glad to have traveled with him. Winks said that whatever Socks decided to do in the future, he couldn't have asked for a better 'bumper.' Hobson wasn't clear what that last bit meant, but Winks told him Socks would understand."

After Socks had gone to bed with the words of praise ringing in his ears, the two older bears lingered in the kitchen. Slippers folded the aired clothes and tidied the hearth. Boots straightened the row of children's shoes and pushed newspaper in the toes to soak up the damp.

"It was good of Winks to remember Socks," said Slippers. "Socks hasn't said anything, but he's sensible enough, and after what happened I know he sees that working full time on the trucks would be too much for him. What Winks said will make all the difference."

Even when the room was tidy, the two bears still lingered in the doorway staring at the banners of Christmas cards on the firelit walls, the Coronation tea caddy between the brass candlesticks on the mantel, and the rag hearthrug Mrs. Trinket had made from the family's discarded clothes.

"If Bret and Hobson and the others hadn't kept their heads, we might be at sea this very minute," said Slippers.

"Or in it," said Boots. "Hannibal said all along that once those thieves found out we weren't new like the rest of the toys it would be all over for us, and Winks ran it pretty close."

Both of them thought of the dreadful minutes they had spent in the bottom of the rowboat. They knew in their hearts that there was one person to whom they owed their safety more than anyone else. If Frank Fielding hadn't confronted the thieves so boldly, all that the others had tried to do might have been lost.

As they climbed slowly up the stairs, Slippers spoke.

"Whatever we may have felt about Frank in the beginning, no one could have done better today. The way he tackled those thieves and stood by Polly when she needed him most was as much as anyone could wish."

Boots took the last three steps on all fours because he was tired after such a difficult day. On the top step he sat down and stared at his back paws. Polly's stitches on one of his chamois pads had come undone, and the tightly curled straw stuffing bulged through. Boots thought of all Polly Trinket's care for them over so many years. Soon she would have Frank

Fielding's pullovers to knit, his socks to darn, and his shirts to mend. When Boots looked up, the moonlight shone through the landing window on his honest face.

"Frank may not be all that we had in mind for Polly," he said, "but now we know what he's made of. Kindness and a stout heart make up for a lot. I think he'll do."

Back in Business

THAT CHRISTMAS it wasn't any of their own presents that the Trinkets remembered ever afterwards but a typewritten letter which arrived for Polly's fiancé on Christmas Eve.

When Frank read the letter at breakfast, he blushed right up to the roots of his red hair and handed it to Polly without saying a word.

"It's from the firm who owned the toy van that was stolen," said Polly, looking up from the letter with shining eyes. "Their insurance company has given Frank a reward of five hundred pounds for helping to recover the Dodge and its contents."

"And now with what we've saved there's nothing in the world to stop us from being married," said Frank. "We'll be able to have a place of our own and to do what we've always planned."

Mrs. Trinket was so surprised the lid of the teapot fell into the cup she was filling. Polly and Frank laughed and cried, and all the Trinkets asked questions at once.

The small house in Station Road was full of excited preparations. Polly Trinket was known and liked throughout Slumber Lightly. The cats brought the bears and Hannibal all the latest news from the town.

"The Bishop's officiating at their wedding himself in the cathedral," Big Tom reported.

"They'll have the organ and the full choir with both Polly's brothers in the front row," said Little Tom.

"The reception is to be in the café where Mrs. Trinket has always worked," said Hobson. "They've put the refreshments at special rates and the manageress has given the cake—"

"—with three tiers and a model of the happy couple under an arch of orange blossom on the top," said Big Tom. "Even the Bishop's niece never had a bigger one."

Wedding presents arrived by every post. Feathers came with a good many on the mail truck, and Upsidaisy brought the larger packages on the parcels truck from the station.

"Feathers says she's never seen so many gifts,"

Socks reported proudly after the mail truck had stopped twice at the house in one day. "Upsidaisy says there's been nothing like it for years."

The front room was crowded with toast racks, blankets, china, a cuckoo clock, saucepans, two plastic washing-up sets, a rolling pin, and a whole set of wooden spoons from Polly's old Brownie Pack, striped bath towels, sets of sheets bordered with rosebuds, and a great many tea towels with such handsome pictures on them that Polly intended to hang them on the walls.

There was an electric cake mixer, a pop-up toaster, a pair of kitchen scales that hung on the wall, and a record player the bears all tried out themselves. The company who owned the shoe shop in Cordwainer's Row gave Polly a spin dryer, which Slippers forbade Socks to touch.

"It's in place of a mangle, and they're dangerous enough," Slippers explained as they stood around the machine. "Frank will show Polly how to use it."

Mrs. Trinket and the children gave Polly a tea-making machine which the bears admired more than all the other gifts.

"You set that alarm clock to the time you want," Boots explained. "Then a bell wakes you up and the machine makes the tea." Even Big Tom and Little Tom came twice to see Boots demonstrate the machine with all the instructions spread out before him.

A week before the wedding, Hobson arrived with a plastic pot scourer for Polly, which had been left over from a free-gift offer with soap powder at his shop.

"The Trinkets have always been free with their milk," the big cat told them, "and I thought it might come in handy."

The bears longed to give Polly something themselves, only there was nothing they could find.

"It wouldn't be expected," Hannibal decided. "Polly would be the last to look for it. Even that pot scourer's caused a good deal of fuss. Polly thought her great-aunt had sent it, and when she thanked her, it turned out she had given an ornamental plant pot and quite a large check."

When Polly's wedding day finally came, mistakes about pot scourers were forgotten. Polly looked as beautiful as any princess when she set out for the cathedral in a large hired automobile decorated with white ribbons. Perched on the front bumper was a black velvet kitten with *Good Luck* printed on a label tied around its neck.

"The cat wasn't anyone I know," said Socks gruffly when Slippers asked as they turned away from the window. "Car mascots mostly keep themselves to themselves. Winks never likes the way they put on airs and bob about in the back windows."

After the bustle of Polly's departure, the house was quiet. The cathedral bells stopped ringing and the bears knew the service had begun.

While Hannibal stood in the hall, the bears wandered around the empty house. In Polly's room her luggage stood ready. Her going-away clothes lay on the bed, with her gloves and handbag, which all matched.

"She'll change here before she leaves with Frank after the reception," Slippers explained as Boots gave Polly's new shoes a final rub with the back of his paw. "They're not having a honeymoon but going straight to their new home in Frank's delivery truck."

Now that all the wedding presents had been packed, the sitting room looked bare. Only a leaflet of washing instructions lay on the sofa, with a length of white ribbon and a crumpled silver label.

"They'll be at the reception now," said Boots, "making speeches and reading out the telegrams."

"The cats promised they'd watch from the skylight over the café and tell us everything about the reception," said Slippers, with her eye on Socks as he fidgeted with the cardboard boxes in which slices of wedding cake would be sent to absent friends.

"And there's bound to be lots about the wedding in the local paper, besides a mention in the *Boot and Shoe Gazette*," said Boots.

Socks didn't look up.

"Hearing about Polly's wedding from everyone else won't be the same," he said. "I wanted to be there. We've known Polly for ages and ages and it's only us who weren't asked."

Socks was near to tears. A white bow hung limp around his neck. One of the wedding-cake boxes lay dented under his paw.

"But we couldn't have been invited," said Slippers, putting her arm around his shoulders. "It wasn't to be expected."

"I did expect it," said Socks. "I expected Polly would ask us, right up to the moment she went off in that car. She's always looked after us, even when we really belonged to Bill and Simon and Audrey. Now they're all too old to need bears any longer, and with Polly gone, no one will bother about us any more. Ever since we went to work at that coal merchant's, we've tried to find something we could do, but nothing's been any use. I liked going on the trucks more than anything else in the world, but after that trip with Winks I knew I couldn't do it always. I should only have been a nuisance, and the others would have had to look after me. We're no use to anybody. Even being sent away to sea would have been better than staying here just to be forgotten and put away in a drawer."

When Socks stopped speaking, the room was silent. Only the clock ticked on the mantel. Slippers saw the three of them reflected in the mirror above the fire-place: Boots with his thinning fur, her own hand-darned nose and mouth and missing ear, the stains on Socks's paws, which even the strongest detergents would never wash out, and she knew Socks's words might be true.

"That's Frank's delivery truck turning the corner now," said Boots. "He's brought Polly with her mother and the children."

The house was suddenly full of laughter and cheer-ful voices as Polly raced up the stairs, accompanied by her mother and Audrey, while Frank waited in the hall with luggage all around him.

Soon the bears heard the last drawer in the bed-room bang shut and Polly scurried downstairs to join Frank in the hall. Listening to all Mrs. Trinket's last-minute questions, Slippers kept her arm around Socks, and Boots didn't speak. They longed for Polly to re-member them just to say goodbye.

"Frank's taken most of the cases out to the delivery truck," Boots reported. "They'll be off in a minute."

"We ought to be in the window," said Slippers. "Polly might look back and like to see us there just as usual."

"Before they could join Boots on the windowsill, Frank called to Polly from the front steps.

"I've got Hannibal, if you'll bring along the bears. It would never do to forget them now."

The door burst open and suddenly they were all in Polly's arms. Her red hair brushed their worn fur as she bent over them, her face bright with happiness. As she bundled them out to the waiting truck, she whispered to them, just as she had always talked to them when they were with her in the shoe shop long ago.

"You'll be needed now more than you've ever been needed before," she told them. "We're all going to be busier than we've ever been in our lives."

Mrs. Trinket and the children waved till the truck, with Hannibal and the bears crowded in the back window, was out of sight.

The bears never forgot their drive. Confetti speckled Frank's dark blue suit, and a silver-paper horseshoe was still tangled in Polly's blowing hair. The bears sat up very straight on the piled luggage. The cold air flattened their fur and lifted Hannibal's saddlecloth so that all the bells tinkled. None of them knew where they were going or what the work was that they would be expected to do. So long as they were with Polly, they didn't care.

Socks identified every truck and van to the others as they passed. Even when Boots and Slippers grew tired, Hannibal listened.

"That's an Austin, that's a Ford, that ten-ton truck's a Bedford, those yellow trucks loaded with gravel are dump trucks, and there's a Commer right behind . . ."

Once or twice Socks caught sight of a battered mascot perched on a truck as it thundered past, and he always waved on the off-chance that it might be one of his old friends.

"You'll be able to keep in touch with Winks and the others, I've no doubt," Hannibal remarked as Socks gazed after a mud-spattered Luton truck till it was out of sight. "Polly's sure to visit her mother in Slumber Lightly quite often. You could always go back with her and look them all up. Though it's rough on the trucks in the winter, a jaunt with Winks in the spring and summer will do you a world of good. Even if you're not able to take up road haulage professionally, nothing could make a better hobby."

Even Socks dozed off at last as the truck bowled on its way. It was almost dark when the bears woke to find themselves driving through the narrow streets of a small town. They saw a church with a shingled spire and a broad market street with small, brightly lit shops on either side. There was a town hall with a clock tower and a bus stop outside. Everything about the town was far smaller than Slumber Lightly. Even the stars and moon seemed closer to the pantiled roofs and rounded chimney stacks, yet somehow it was the same. A gray British Blue cat sat in the doorway of the bank; they saw a ginger cat asleep in the lighted window above the hardware dealer's; a plump black Persian sat washing the back of her front paw outside a shop which sold dry goods and hats; two young tabbies scurried up the pleached lime-tree walk that led to the church.

The delivery truck slowed down and swung off the main street into a narrow courtyard. Ahead of them, the bears saw a white-painted bow-windowed shop with curtained windows above. In the shop window were red-buckled shoes, dancing slippers, blue, red, and black boots, bedroom slippers, walking shoes, sandals, and brocaded party slippers.

"They're all small sizes, especially for children," Slippers whispered as the van halted outside.

"And look at the sign painted over the shop window," said Boots. "It says:

CHILDREN'S SHOE SHOP
Joint Proprietors, Frank and Polly Fielding

That's why Polly needs us so much, and this is where we'll go back to our old work."

The shop fitted the bears as comfortably as a hand-sewn shoe. In the showroom, white paint decorated the paneled walls. The broad floorboards were waxed and all the fittings were dark blue. At the back of the shop was a blackleaded hob grate, and beside it stood a basket chair.

"The bears look at home already," said Polly as she left them in the chair with Hannibal beside them. "I'm sure they'll help make our shop a success."

"Of course they will," said her husband. "We couldn't have asked for anything better."

Late that night, Socks lay half asleep with Slippers and Boots in the basket chair. Socks knew that Winks and Joshua, Watchit and Feathers, Upsidaisy and Fly-over would be along when the spring came. And when he visited Station Road with Hannibal and the other bears, while Boots and Slippers entertained Hobson and their other old friends among the cats of Slumber Lightly in the kitchen, he would slip away to the station yard. Aloft once more with Winks on the hood of the Dodge, there would be fresh journeys to make and places to explore.

As the moonlight shone across the neatly stacked shoe boxes, the blue leather tops of the fitting stools, and the chairs set ready for the first customers, the bears slept, knowing that their long search was over. They had found work to do that they all understood. Their retirement had ended and they were back in business.